ENDS OF THE EARTH

THE WORLD'S REMOTE AND WILD PLACES

The Kimberley

Debbie Gallagher

Heinemann
LIBRARY

© 1997 Ogma Writers

Published by Heinemann Library

an imprint of Reed Educational & Professional Publishing

500 Coventry Lane

Crystal Lake, IL 60014

Library of Congress Cataloging-in-Publication Data

Gallagher, Debbie, 1969-
  The Kimberley / Debbie Gallagher.
    p. cm. -- (Ends of the earth)
  Includes index.
  Summary: Describes the geography, wildlife, and people, including more than thirty distinct groups of Aborigines, of the Kimberley region of Western Australia.
  ISBN 0-431-06933-6 (lib. bdg.)
  1. Kimberley (W.A.)--Juvenile literature. [1. Kimberley (W.A.) 2. Australia.]
I. Title. II. Series.
DU380.K5G35 1997
994.1'4--DC21
                                                97-1928
                                                  CIP
                                                   AC

01 00 99 98 97

10 9 8 7 6 5 4 3 2 1

Designed by David Doyle and Irwin Liaw

Edited by Stephen Dobney

Front cover photograph by Mike Leonard

Back cover photograph by Neil Maclean

Picture research by Ogma Writers

Illustrations by Andrew Plant

Production by Elena Cementon

Printed in Hong Kong by H&Y Printing Limited

Contents

Introduction

Imagine a corner of the world so remote that it feels like no one has ever been there, where the sky stretches to horizons that seem as far away as they can get. This is the Kimberley, a region of dramatic mountain ranges, flat-topped rock platforms (mesas), deep gorges, spectacular waterfalls, and vast plateaus.

The Kimberley covers the whole top part of Western Australia, from the steep cliffs and ragged coastline in the north and west where there are 25 to 40 foot tides, to the Ord River in the east, and the Great Sandy Desert in the south. In this area of about 160,000 square miles live some 20,000 people, 40 percent of whom are Aborigines.

Roads in the region are few and have been built mainly for the flourishing cattle industry. Most are impassable during the wet season. Broome, on the southern coast of the Dampier Peninsula, is the region's largest town. Derby and Wyndham are also located on or near the coast, at the edges of the Kimberley. Inland, the smaller towns of Turkey Creek, Halls Creek, and Fitzroy Crossing are spread along the Great Northern Highway between Kununurra and Broome.

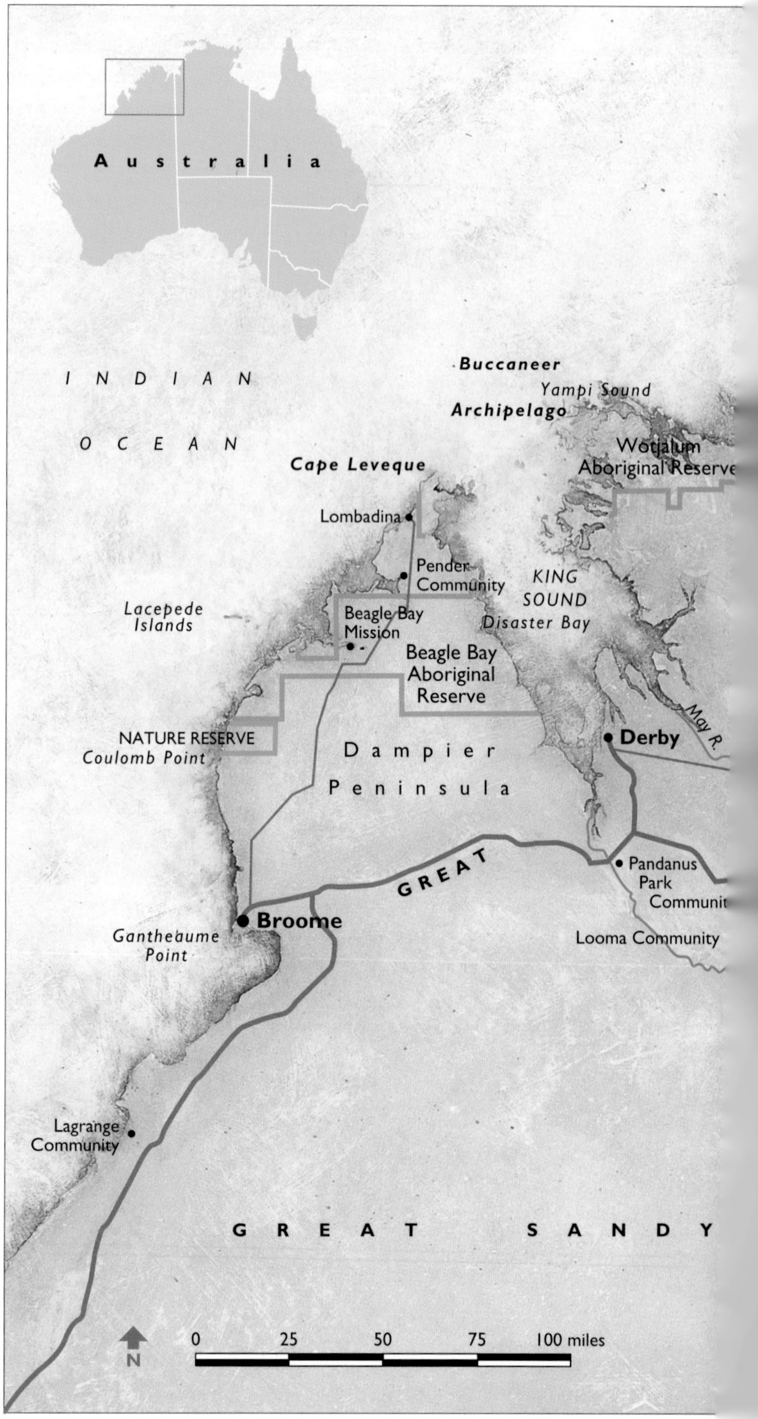

Figure 1 The Kimberley.

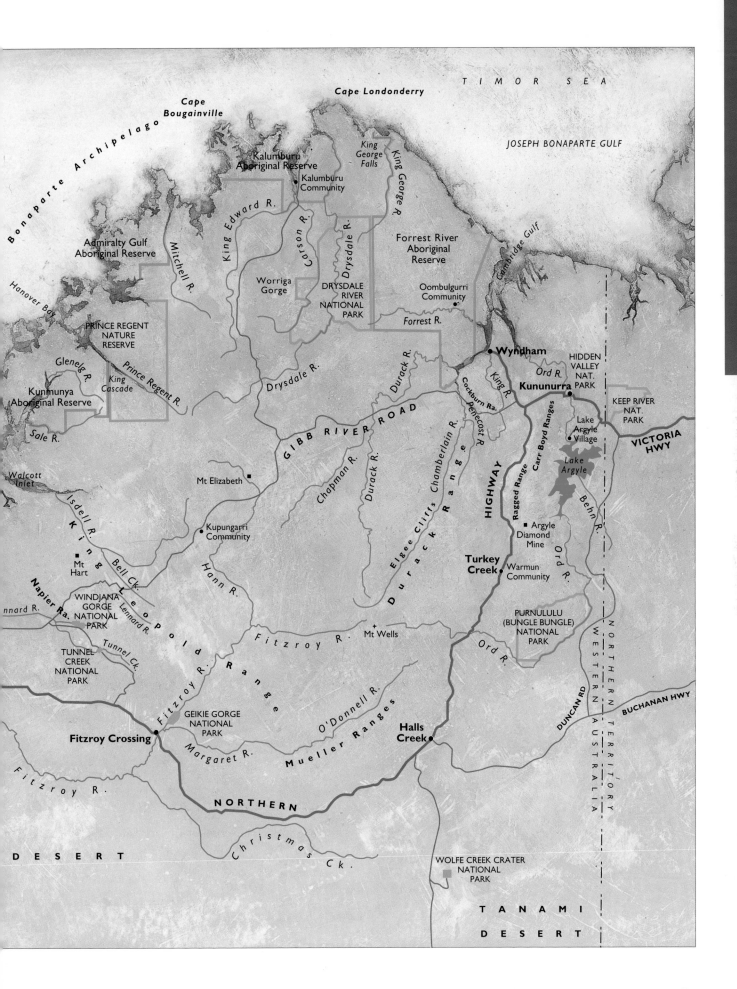

TIMOR SEA

Cape Londonderry

Cape
Bougainville

JOSEPH BONAPARTE GULF

Bonaparte Archipelago

King George Falls

Kalumburu
Aboriginal Reserve

Kalumburu
Community

King George R.

Admiralty Gulf
Aboriginal Reserve

King Edward R.

Carson R.

Drysdale R.

Forrest River
Aboriginal Reserve

Cambridge Gulf

Mitchell R.

Worriga
Gorge

DRYSDALE
RIVER
NATIONAL
PARK

Oombulgurri
Community

Hanover Bay

PRINCE
REGENT
NATURE
RESERVE

Forrest R.

Wyndham

HIDDEN
VALLEY
NAT.
PARK

Prince Regent R.

Glenelg R.

Drysdale R.

Ord R.

Kununurra

King
Cascade

Drysdale R.

Durack R.

Cockburn Ra.

King R.

KEEP RIVER
NAT. PARK

Kunmunya
Aboriginal Reserve

Pentecost R.

Carr Boyd Ranges

Lake
Argyle
Village

VICTORIA
HWY

Sale R.

GIBB RIVER ROAD

Chapman R.

Elgee Cliffs

Chamberlain R.

Ragged Range

Lake
Argyle

Walcott
Inlet

Mt Elizabeth

Durack R.

Behn R.

HIGHWAY

Isdell R.

Kupungarri
Community

Durack Range

Argyle
Diamond
Mine

King Leopold Range

Bell Ck.

Hann R.

Turkey
Creek

Warmun
Community

Mt
Hart

Napier Ra.

WINDJANA
GORGE
NATIONAL
PARK

Lennard R.

PURNULULU
(BUNGLE BUNGLE)
NATIONAL
PARK

nnard R.

Fitzroy R.

Mt Wells

Ord R.

TUNNEL
CREEK
NATIONAL
PARK

Tunnel Ck.

O'Donnell R.

Mueller Ranges

DUNCAN RD

BUCHANAN HWY

GEIKIE GORGE
NATIONAL
PARK

Halls
Creek

WESTERN AUSTRALIA

NORTHERN TERRITORY

Fitzroy Crossing

Fitzroy R.

Margaret R.

Fitzroy R.

NORTHERN

Christmas Ck.

DESERT

WOLFE CREEK CRATER
NATIONAL
PARK

TANAMI

DESERT

5

National parks

The Kimberley is an extremely rugged region, and large parts of it remain virtually inaccessible. Several nature reserves and national parks have been established to protect the environment and provide opportunities for people to explore the region.

The Bungle Bungle Range

In the southeast corner of the Kimberley is the Purnululu (Bungle Bungle) National Park, which is renowned for its anthill-shaped rock formations. Known by the Kija Aborigines as Purnululu, meaning sandstone, the area was probably given the name Bungle Bungle Range by Arthur Muggleton, who leased it for cattle grazing from 1929 to 1937. The area was used

(Photo courtesy of Neil Macleod)

Figure 2 This is the sight that attracts thousands of visitors to the Bungle Bungle Range. These dome-shaped hills form a series of palm-lined gorges dotted with isolated pools.

by pastoralists up until the late 1960s when the government reclaimed much of it, as it badly needed rehabilitation. In 1987, half a million acres were set aside as the Purnululu National Park, and a further 275,000 acres were set aside as a nature reserve.

Cathedral Gorge, which can be reached reasonably easily by walking along a creek bed, is the most visited part of the park. Piccaninny Gorge is far more spectacular, however, showing off the conical orange and black domes that make this park unique. The remainder of the park consists of wide plains of acacia shrubs, spinifex grass, and eucalyptus trees.

Figure 3 Drysdale River National Park is so large and hard to reach that not even park officials knew much about it until it was surveyed in 1975.

Figure 4 The Solea Falls in the Drysdale River National Park. "Solea," which is Latin for horseshoe, well describes the shape of this spectacular waterfall.

Drysdale River—the untouched park

Drysdale River National Park, 100 miles west of Wyndham, is inaccessible by road and remains an almost untouched corner of wilderness. It is Western Australia's northernmost national park and, at one million acres, is also the largest. The park is mostly open woodland with the broad Drysdale River cutting through the middle. Tall trees grow along many of the river and creek banks. The Solea Falls in the north and the Morgan Falls in the west are among the most beautiful waterfalls in the Kimberley.

The park also has several pockets of rainforest, the most notable being along the Carson Escarpment and in the Worriga Gorge. The 600 recorded plant species found in the park include many that are unique to the area. Of the 25 fern species, half are found only in the Worriga Gorge.

Mirima—the hidden valley

The Mirima National Park, also known as Hidden Valley because of its many gorges and winding valleys, is just two miles east of Kununurra. Hidden Valley Road winds between steep walls to Lily Creek which, together with its tributaries, has cut valleys through layers of ancient rock. This is the most visited national park in the Kimberley, popular not only with tourists but also with Kununurra residents. It is an area of rock wallabies, eucalyptuses and baobabs, sheer cliffs, and more of the strange "bungle bungle" formations.

The Purnululu Echidna

The Aborigines of the Bungle Bungle Range tell a story about how the strange rock domes were created. One day a galah (cockatoo) and an echidna (spiny anteater) had a fight. When the galah swooped down, the echidna tried to hide. First he dug one hole, then another, until the whole area was covered in mounds and hollows. But the galah kept getting closer. Finally the echidna raised up all his sharp quills to scare her off, but to his dismay they all fell out. The quills scattered all around the mounds and grew into tall palm trees. That is how Purnululu was formed.

The gorge parks

The three tiny national parks at Tunnel Creek, Geikie Gorge, and Windjana Gorge offer spectacular glimpses of the southern Kimberley Ranges.

Windjana Gorge National Park

Windjana Gorge is a narrow 2.5-mile-long canyon located about two hours drive from Derby. The Lennard River flows across an open floodplain into the walls of the gorge which rise as high as 325 feet. During the wet season, the river flows hard and fast, but when the rains stop it becomes a series of deep pools often inhabited by freshwater crocodiles.

The canyon walls are covered with clumps of spinifex and rock figs. Caves in the gorge contain Aboriginal rock paintings dating back thousands of years. On the floor of the gorge grow tall Leichhardt trees, native figs, and tropical paperbarks, which are favorites with the waterbirds, corellas, and fruit bats.

Figure 5

(Photo courtesy of Maria Mann)

(Photo courtesy of Neil Macleod)

Figure 6 (left) The towering walls of Windjana Gorge form a small section of the Napier Range. Around 350 million years ago, the rocks you see here were part of a huge, living barrier reef beneath the sea. The sea level dropped and, over millions of years, a river cut a path through the reef to create the present gorge.

Tunnel Creek National Park

To the southeast is Tunnel Creek, a huge, natural tunnel carved 2500 feet into the Napier Range. During the dry season a path leads through the cool, dark tunnel past the homes of ghost and fruit bats to a roof collapse in the middle of the tunnel where the hot, tropical sunlight streams down once again. Freshwater crocodiles can also be found in some of the permanent pools along the river.

Figure 7

(Photo courtesy of Neil Macleod)

Geikie Gorge National Park

Geikie Gorge is regarded as the most beautiful of the Kimberley gorges and, at 5 miles, it is also the longest. It was named "Geikie" in 1883 after a British geologist, but its traditional name is Darngku. The Fitzroy River changes from a raging torrent in the wet to a vast waterhole in the dry, when boat trips and riverside walks become possible. Parts of the park have been reserved as wildlife sanctuaries for the short-eared rock wallabies, orange horseshoe bats, and the many types of birds, including the rare lilac-crowned wren and the white-breasted sea eagle.

The Bunaba Aborigines are very much involved in the region, providing boat tours along the river and helping to run a backpackers' hostel.

Figure 8

(Photo courtesy of Maria Mann)

Geikie's ghost

A story of the Bunaba Aborigines tells of a blind Aboriginal elder who lived in the gorge during the Dreamtime. When he left the tribe to go wandering he drowned in the gorge, sighing and sneezing till he sank for the last time. They say you can still hear his sighs when the gorge is quiet.

The unknown Kimberley

The lack of roads and the region's small population mean that many of the Kimberley's unique geological features remain much the way they were thousands of years ago. Because of this isolation, there have been no known extinctions of plants or animals in the northern Kimberley since Europeans arrived on the continent 200 years ago. To make sure this continues, the government has set aside large tracts of land as nature reserves, and permits are required to enter these areas. Many of the nature reserves and other beauty spots are extremely difficult to get to, and some can be seen only from the air.

Pelican Island Nature Reserve in the Joseph Bonaparte Gulf (named after Napoleon's brother) was established to protect Australian pelicans during their breeding season. Another island, Lacepede, is an important seabird and turtle reserve. Parry Lagoon's Nature Reserve is 12 miles south of Wyndham, while Coulomb Point, north of Broome, is the only area where the unique pindan vegetation of the Dampier Peninsula is protected.

Prince Regent Nature Reserve

The Prince Regent Nature Reserve, 1,500,000 acres of wilderness in the highest rainfall area of the Kimberley, is not accessible by road. Inside its boundaries can be found the King Cascades

Figure 9 The Mitchell Falls are one of the most spectacular waterfalls in the Kimberley, but very few people get to see them because of their isolation.

Figure 10 (left) The goanna is Australia's largest lizard, or monitor, and is found in many parts of the Kimberley. Despite its fierce appearance, it tends to be shy rather than dangerous.

Figure 11 (above)   The Elgee Cliffs run north for 75 miles along the Chamberlain River, forming a single, unbroken escarpment.

(a magnificent 100-foot-long waterfall discovered by Captain King in 1820), the Python Cliffs, and the Prince Regent River, which flows between near-vertical cliffs.

The Prince Regent reserve is particularly rich in flora and fauna, containing more than half the total number of mammal species as well as half the number of bird species known in the Kimberley. More than 500 plant species have also been discovered. Management of the reserve includes controlling feral animals and fires. Saltwater crocodiles, whose numbers were badly depleted by hunting, are now flourishing in the region thanks to this protection.

The Kimberley coast

The Kimberley may have a tiny human population, but it supports a magnificent and diverse range of animal and plant life.

Mangroves

An important feature of the Kimberley coast is the mangrove forest that greets the flow of the Ord and Fitzroy rivers as they empty into the sea. Up to 15 species of mangrove have been listed in the Kimberley, and they support a wide variety of life.

Mangroves survive best along river estuaries and in sheltered areas where they are protected from powerful currents. They grow in salt water, in the inter-tidal zone. The roots of the mangroves play an important part in holding the coastlines intact and reducing the effect of sea currents. Different types of mangroves can often be identified by their roots, as well as by where they grow.

The white mangrove grows closest to the sea, its roots growing out of the swampy mud. At low tide, small holes in the roots take in essential supplies of oxygen, which are stored while the roots are submerged at high tide. In the center of the mangrove forest, grows the stilt-rooted mangrove. Its roots grow down from stems and branches above the ground. As with the white mangrove, the roots prevent salt from destroying the plants. The roots of the yellow-leafed spurred mangrove grow downward at angles from the trunk to support the tree, and are called "prop roots."

Crabs, shellfish, bats, and birds are all part of the mangrove ecosystem. Oysters can be found clinging to the roots of mangroves. Crabs do their part by digging in the mud, allowing oxygen to reach buried roots. Shellfish devour the leaves that fall from the mangroves, while bats and birds pollinate the trees, ensuring their survival. In turn the mangroves supply birds such as the heron and the kite with a steady supply of insects and crabs.

(Photo courtesy of Neil Macleod)

Figure 12 Looking north across the Napier Broome Bay, north of Kalumburu, where the King Edward River meets the sea. Mangrove swamps and mud flats stretch in all directions.

Figure 13 (left)   There are 21 species of crocodiles in the world, but only two are found in Australia: the saltwater (estuarine) crocodile and the freshwater crocodile. Both species are protected in the Kimberley. Saltwater crocodiles such as this one live in the mangrove-lined tidal estuaries, occasionally making their way upriver. Visitors have died by wandering too close to crocodile habitat.

Figure 14 (below)   The mud crab lives in and around the mangroves, and is an essential part of the mangrove ecosystem. As it burrows in the mud it allows oxygen to reach the roots. The mangroves, in turn, attract oysters which cling to their roots and are eaten by the mud crabs.

Figure 15 (above)   White or gray mangroves are the most common of the mangrove plants. The leaves of the mangrove have special organs, or glands, that remove salt from the plant.

Dugongs and crocodiles

One of the most fascinating of the coastal creatures is the dugong. This dolphin-like creature can live for up to 70 years and can grow up to 10 feet long. Female dugongs have calves only once every few years. This means that their habitat must be carefully protected or they could face extinction.

The most awe-inspiring creature of the Kimberley coast is the saltwater (estuarine) crocodile. Despite their name, these crocodiles can be found up to 60 miles inland. In ancient times the Aborigines painted pictures of them on the rock walls of the Kimberley, and today the legend of the crocodile still looms large.

These creatures may be more than 23 feet long and weigh up to a ton. They don't chew their prey, they crush it, rip it apart and swallow it whole. The crocodile's ability to store the food it swallows means that it may only need to feed once a week.

The rivers

The Fitzroy River in the southwest and the Ord River in the northeast are the two great river systems of the Kimberley. Numerous tributaries flow out from them, and the two rivers almost meet in the Kimberley's southeast. In the dry season these rivers cease to flow, but do not completely dry up. In the wet season, however, they become powerful and dangerous as enormous amounts of water surge toward the sea. They have been a hindrance to exploration, yet they are a vital source of life to the habitats of the Kimberley.

River fish

One of the great attractions of the Kimberley's rivers is the silver-gray barramundi, which can often be heard at night as it pursues and "chomps" at its prey of small fish on the water's surface. Barramundi can grow over three feet in length and some fishers have claimed to have caught fish weighing up to 110 pounds. All young barramundi are male. As the fish grow, some become female while others remain male. The annual flooding of the rivers is essential to the life cycle of the barramundi, which need the flow of water to hurdle over obstacles as they make their way upriver. The barramundi prefer the deeper parts of the river away from the banks.

The archerfish is another fascinating creature of the Kimberley's rivers. This fish prowls near the surface of the water or close to

(Photo courtesy of Ken Stepnell)

the banks under overhanging branches. The fish fires an "arrow" of water at unsuspecting insects and spiders, knocking them into the water to be devoured.

The river red gum

Numerous varieties of trees line the banks of the Kimberley's rivers, in places opening into areas of rainforest. The most impressive of these is the white-trunked river red gum which can rise to a

Figure 17 (left) The Ord River changes from being slow and gentle in the dry season (as shown here), to a raging torrent in the wet, carrying huge amounts of silt. These characteristics made the river very difficult to control but, after careful planning, a dam was completed in 1972. The dam includes special features to accommodate the huge variations in water volume and to prevent the new lake being filled with silt.

Figure 18 (left) Not much was known about the Drysdale River until 1975 when an expedition was sent to carry out scientific exploration. It was noted that the river system supported around 600 different plants and 2500 animal species. Here the Drysdale River is seen in the wet season.

Figure 16 (left) The Ord River is an essential source of fresh water for plants, animals, and people in the Kimberley. In the wet season it drains an area of 16,000 square miles. This is a spillway stream that carries runoff from the Ord River Dam.

The "freshie"

Lurking beneath the water's surface is that other attraction to Australia's north, the freshwater crocodile. The "freshie," as it is known, is found not only in rivers, but also in creeks, billabongs, and wetlands. Males can grow up to 10 feet long, while females grow to around 6 feet.

Freshies are not as dangerous as their saltwater cousins, but nevertheless they should not be cornered or harassed. The crocodile weighs its body down in the water by swallowing stones. Only its eyes and the tip of its snout are left to peer out of the water, as the croc patiently awaits its next victim. The crocodile clutches the victim (perhaps a white bream) in its sharp teeth and, with a flick of its head, throws the fish to the back of its mouth where it is crushed and swallowed.

height of 80 feet. The long, narrow leaves that droop from its branches contain eucalyptus oil which protects them from most animals and insects. The bark of the river red gum peels off, sometimes revealing a surprising inhabitant— the bardi grub—which makes its home in the wood. The bardi grub is a traditional source of "bush tucker." Another food source along the Kimberley rivers is the wild plum tree. Both the fruit and the gum of this tree can be eaten.

The wet and the dry

The arid zone

Like the rest of northern Australia, the Kimberley does not have a summer or a winter, but rather a wet season and a dry season. Within these seasons the climate varies across the Kimberley: the northwest is hot and humid in the "summer" months while the southeastern region is hot and dry. In the "winter," all the Kimberley is dry.

Kimberley Aborigines have identified as many as seven different seasonal conditions. *Wundju* is the height of the wet season, when plants and animals are most scarce. *Yirma*, from May through to August, is the beginning of the dry, and plants and animals are more numerous.

Dotting the dry regions of the Kimberley is a small thick-trunked tree called the baobab.

(Photo courtesy of Rodney Paterson)

Figure 19 Lizards and other reptiles are well suited to the arid parts of the Kimberley. Spinifex provides the shelter, and termites provide the food for several types of lizard.

This tree discards its leaves in the dry season to retain vital moisture in its soft brown wood. Its leafless branches reach up to the sky as though awaiting the next rains.

The baobab, standing alone and independent, is one of the great symbols of the Kimberley. It is a sign of life in the arid expanses of the Kimberley during the dry season. It is also a surprisingly useful tree: the Aborigines used its gum for glue, its bark for twine and its seeds for food.

Spinifex grows all year round and protects the desert soil from being blown or washed away. The spinifex is a friend to many animal species in the dry regions, and is the nesting place of the spinifex bird. The fork-tailed kite keeps cool by spreading its wings and keeping its beak open. When fire breaks out on the plains, the kites fly over the fire, ready to pounce on the animals and insects fleeing the flames.

Rainforest

In the middle of the arid Kimberley there are more than 1500 pockets of rainforest, ranging in size from just a few trees up to 250 acres. These are reminders of the region's ancient past when the Kimberley, like most of the continent, was very wet. The fossilized remains of vast rainforests can be found throughout the area, but the pockets of living rainforest were known only to local Aborigines until 1965.

Figure 20 (above)   Even in the driest areas of the Kimberley, green vegetation can surprisingly appear. Rain flowing off the rocks of the Cockburn Ranges has created a fertile patch of green bushland that contrasts with the red cliffs.

Clever adaptations

The animals of this arid region have had to adapt to survive. The little marsupial mouse known as the striped-faced dunnart survives the dry winters by storing fat in its long tail. Other animals, such as the red kangaroo and the bilby (a small desert creature) don't sweat, which means they don't lose moisture. The red kangaroo licks its forelegs to cool them down.

The desert is the ideal home for lizards, which burrow into the ground to keep cool, and snakes such as the desert death adder which find shade beneath the many varieties of spinifex grass. The body of the thorny devil (a type of lizard) is covered with hundreds of "thorns." The grooves between the thorns channel any water that lands on the lizard's body to the corners of its mouth.

Figure 21   The baobab is one of the symbols of the Kimberley. It presents a mystery for scientists because several other species of baobab are found in southern Africa. Two possible explanations have been proposed. Either the lands of Africa and Australia were once joined, forming part of the ancient landmass known as Pangaea, or seeds from the island of Madagascar were carried across the sea millions of years ago and took root in the Kimberley. This giant baobab tree, near Derby, was once used as a temporary prison.

An ancient land

Not only is the Kimberley one of the least known and most rugged parts of Australia, but it is also one of the most ancient corners of the world. The region is dominated by the Kimberley Plateau, an area of over 60,000 square miles sitting on a bed of flat sandstone, shale, and volcanic rock, which was formed when ancient volcanoes spewed lava over the land.

It was during the Pre-Cambrian era, which began 4500 million years ago, that the rocks that make up the Kimberley landscape began to be formed. This process lasted some 150 million years. As the sea level rose, water covered the area and eroded the rocks, creating sediment that formed the huge basins of the Kimberley.

The last period of intense mountain building took place 1700 million years ago, and little geological change has occurred since that time.

Most of the rocks you see in the Kimberley today are 400 million years old. In comparison, the Himalayas, which were formed when the subcontinent of India collided with Asia, are only 4 million years old, and the oldest parts of the ocean floor are 100 million years old.

Evidence can still be seen of two glacial periods which occurred 750 and 670 million years ago. The pathways of ancient glaciers (known as "glacial pavements") found in the eastern Kimberley are among the best examples in the world. Geologists believe that massive bolders, which have been found some 30 miles away from the nearest outcrop of "parent" rock, were transported by such glaciers. The highly polished pebbles that can be found in Moonlight Valley provide further evidence that glaciers once helped to shape the landforms of the Kimberley.

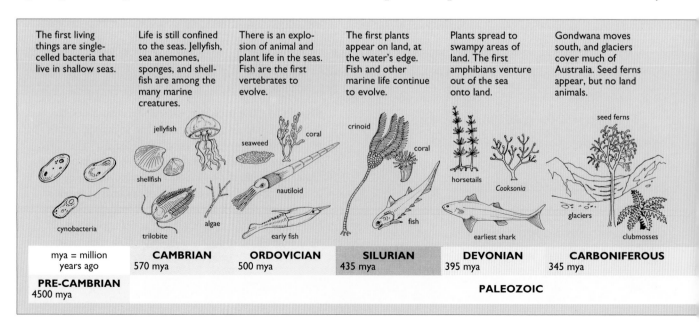

The first living things are single-celled bacteria that live in shallow seas.	Life is still confined to the seas. Jellyfish, sea anemones, sponges, and shellfish are among the many marine creatures.	There is an explosion of animal and plant life in the seas. Fish are the first vertebrates to evolve.	The first plants appear on land, at the water's edge. Fish and other marine life continue to evolve.	Plants spread to swampy areas of land. The first amphibians venture out of the sea onto land.	Gondwana moves south, and glaciers cover much of Australia. Seed ferns appear, but no land animals.

mya = million years ago	CAMBRIAN 570 mya	ORDOVICIAN 500 mya	SILURIAN 435 mya	DEVONIAN 395 mya	CARBONIFEROUS 345 mya
PRE-CAMBRIAN 4500 mya			PALEOZOIC		

Figure 22 There is evidence that the Bungle Bungle Range was hit by a large meteorite at some time. The only remnant is a very shallow depression, the crater walls having been eroded away. Further evidence is found in the sandstone rock around Piccaninny Gorge, which has been heat strengthened. As a result it doesn't wear away grain by grain, but collapses along fractures and forms huge cliffs.

Figure 23 (below)   This geological timeline shows how the Kimberley's landforms and lifeforms have evolved over millions of years, beginning in the Pre-Cambrian era 4500 million years ago.

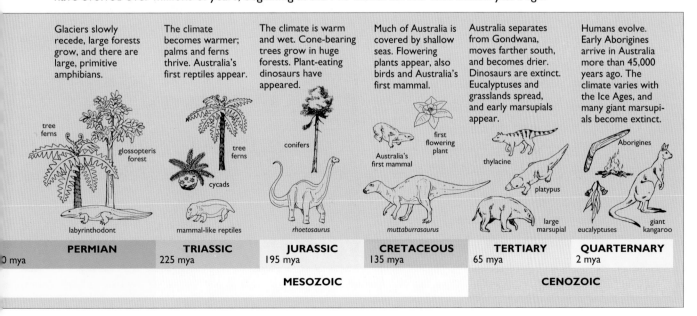

Glaciers slowly recede, large forests grow, and there are large, primitive amphibians.

The climate becomes warmer; palms and ferns thrive. Australia's first reptiles appear.

The climate is warm and wet. Cone-bearing trees grow in huge forests. Plant-eating dinosaurs have appeared.

Much of Australia is covered by shallow seas. Flowering plants appear, also birds and Australia's first mammal.

Australia separates from Gondwana, moves farther south, and becomes drier. Dinosaurs are extinct. Eucalyptuses and grasslands spread, and early marsupials appear.

Humans evolve. Early Aborigines arrive in Australia more than 45,000 years ago. The climate varies with the Ice Ages, and many giant marsupials become extinct.

tree ferns

glossopteris forest

tree ferns

cycads

conifers

first flowering plant

Australia's first mammal

thylacine

platypus

Aborigines

labyrinthodont

mammal-like reptiles

rhoetosaurus

muttaburrasaurus

large marsupial

eucalyptuses

giant kangaroo

PERMIAN	TRIASSIC	JURASSIC	CRETACEOUS	TERTIARY	QUARTERNARY
0 mya	225 mya	195 mya	135 mya	65 mya	2 mya

MESOZOIC

CENOZOIC

A much warmer Kimberley

Around 370 million years ago, during the Devonian period, the Kimberley experienced a warmer climate, and was largely covered by a tropical sea. Under this sea, marine creatures formed a barrier reef up to 600 miles long. Over several million years this reef grew to more than 6500 feet thick. Today it can be seen rising 330 feet or more above the Kimberley plains in the Napier, Lawford, and Oscar Ranges and, on a much smaller scale, at Ningbing Limestone north of Kununurra. The exposed remains of the ancient reef are most visible at the Windjana Gorge in the Napier Range.

After experiencing a cold period which lasted some 150 million years, the Kimberley has remained a warm region for the past 100 million years. Warm-climate dinosaurs lived in the area, as shown by footprints found at Gantheaume Point outside Broome. Up until 30 million years ago the region was also much wetter—wet enough to support vast rainforests. During this time, changes in climate caused a large amount of weathering, so that by the end of the Mesozoic era the Bonaparte, Ord, and Canning Basins were fairly well formed.

The sand dunes along the southern edge of the region were formed during the dry conditions that have prevailed over the last few hundred thousand years. The last very dry period took place 20,000 years ago. The sea was 330 feet lower than it is today, which made the coastline 125 miles farther out. When the polar caps started melting, the sea rose again and flooded the lowlands, producing the spectacular cliffs and numerous steep-walled islands along the coastline. Narrow inlets, such as Walcott Inlet at the western end of the King Leopold Range, are actually drowned valleys.

The Carr Boyd and Cockburn Ranges in the heart of the Kimberley Basin have massive cliffs. The older sandstone from which they are made has been tightly cemented so that it fractures in huge slabs instead of eroding grain by grain. There are also quite a few flat-topped mesas in this area, where the sandstone bedding is almost horizontal.

(Photo courtesy of Rodney Paterson)

Figure 24

Figure 25 (left)   Together with the Napier Range (see Figure 5), the Oscar Range is the remains of an ancient barrier reef that was created during the Devonian period, millions of years ago.

Figure 26 (right)   The Chamberlain River flows north through the eastern Kimberley into Cambridge Gulf. Over time the river has cut a spectacular gorge, revealing the many layers of rock.

The Ragged Range, 60 miles north of the Bungle Bungles, is made up of conglomerate and sandstone towers. At its northern end is a single, huge sand dune. The nearest other sand dunes are 120 miles away to the south. Its age and how it was formed remain a mystery.

Kimberley's oldest inhabitants

When Europeans first came to the Kimberley region there were frequent conflicts with the Aborigines, resulting in deaths on both sides. Since that time, several groups have died out entirely, languages have been lost, and the close bond Aborigines have with the land has been damaged.

Just as the Kimberley is not one single landform, the Aborigines of the Kimberley are not one people. They are the Worrorra or the Bardi, or perhaps the Wunambal, or one of the other 30 or so different groups of Aborigines, each with its own language.

Before European settlement, each group lived in its own distinct territory which was determined by its natural resources—its ability to sustain the group. The Bardi, for instance, are coastal people. The excellent resources along the coast of the Dampier Peninsula meant that they rarely had to travel far to find food and other

necessities. Other groups were more nomadic, ranging over much larger and less fertile areas. Yet others lived along the inland river systems. The boundaries between groups were clearly defined, and people were very careful not to cross group boundaries, in some cases for fear of being killed.

The oldest Aboriginal site in the Kimberley dates back 24,000 years, but the first Aborigines probably arrived in the Kimberley more than 40,000 years ago. One reason why no sites of that age have been found is because the coastline of that time now lies 500 feet beneath

(Photo courtesy of Neil Macleod)

The Aboriginal concept of "belonging" reflects the people's relationship with the land. For Aborigines, people are not the only conscious beings in the environment. Waterholes, animals, and even rocks have names and spirits, and share a common ancestry with the people. This is reflected in Aboriginal artwork and in the concept of the Dreamtime.

Figure 27 Since the days of the "Cattle Kings" (see page 30), many Kimberley Aborigines have worked on the cattle stations that form one of the region's main industries.

the ocean, 150 miles out to sea from the present coastline.

Trade routes linked the various groups of Aborigines in the Kimberley, as well groups beyond the region. In the western part of the Kimberley, these routes were known as *wunan*, and in the east, *winan*. Food, religious objects, and even women were traded on these routes. Boomerangs found their way from the south to the north where they were used for ceremonial purposes, being of little practical benefit to the northern Aborigines.

Figure 28 For most of the period since European settlement, Aboriginal culture and traditions were ignored and destroyed as settlers took over Aboriginal land. Events such as this procession in Broome aim to educate people about the importance of culture to Aboriginal people.

The story of Jundumurra

As the European settlers pushed into the Kimberley to establish towns and cattle stations during the 1890s, the Aborigines who lived there were forced off their hunting grounds and onto the stations as workers. An Aboriginal man named Jundumurra, also known as Pigeon, worked with the Europeans and became a highly skilled horse-man and marksman. During a patrol with the police, Jundumurra was forced to track down 16 Aborigines, but he later shot one of the police officers, took the guns and set the captives free. From then on Jundumurra and his followers lived in hideouts, including one at Tunnel Creek, and battled the white settlers in an effort to defend their land and people. The Europeans finally killed Jundumurra at Tunnel Creek early in 1897.

Figure 29 (above) Bonnie Edwards is a Kimberley Aborigine who is active in the local community. She feels that Aborigines must have a say in the management of the region's national parks in order to protect their heritage.

Rock art

The ancient Aborigines did not leave behind any great buildings. However, throughout the Kimberley there are fascinating remains of ancient Aboriginal rock artwork. Although faded by the passage of time and the relentless onslaught of natural forces, much of the artwork still dominates its surroundings with its impressive sense of life.

On discovering some rock art, the early explorer Sir George Grey wrote that it "appeared to stand out from the rock; and I was certainly rather surprised at the moment that I saw this gigantic head and upper part of a body bending over and grimly staring at me." Grey had come across the Wandjina.

(Photo courtesy of Maria Mann)

Figure 30 To the Aborigines, rock art is not something to be locked up and viewed in a museum. It is a continual expression of the people's relationship with the land and the spirits of the Dreaming. Rock painting continues today in the Kimberley, both in the retouching of ancient rock art and in the expression of new ideas.

The Wandjina

The paintings of the Wandjina are the resting places of the great spirits themselves. Having come from the sky, the Wandjina created many of the features of the Kimberley landscape. They are the source of life: they bring the life-giving seasonal rains, the gift of children, and success in hunting. At the end of their time on Earth, the Wandjina merged with the rocks where they now live.

Aborigines are careful to maintain the favor of the Wandjina spirits. On approaching the paintings, a visitor must cry out so as not to take the spirits by surprise. During each wet season their figures are repainted, renewing the bond between human and spirit. Their stories are retold and sometimes new stories are introduced through a spirit's guardian, usually an Aboriginal elder.

The Kimberley Dynamic Figures

The Wandjina paintings are not the only form of rock art in the Kimberley. Joseph Bradshaw, exploring the Kimberley around 1890, came across a series of drawings which have become known as the Kimberley Dynamic Figures. These are drawings of elongated human figures, sometimes life-size, swaying and stretching across the walls of shelters and caves. They show tools and weapons that have not been used by Aborigines for at least 3000 years. In many

Figure 31 (left)   These stretched out figures painted on the rock are known as Kimberley Dynamic Figures. They are called "dynamic" because of the sense of movement they evoke, like smoke rising into the air or the leaves of a palm tree gently swaying in the wind. They are mostly found in the northwest of the Kimberley.

Figure 32 (below)   The paintings of the Wandjina are the resting places of the great spirits themselves.

Miriwun rock shelter

When Charles Dortch of the Western Australia Museum excavated a site now under the waters of Lake Argyle, he uncovered a campsite at least 18,000 years old, making it one of the oldest sites showing human activity. Finely made stone spear points found on the site date back at least 5000 years. The Kimberley region is known for these spear points, which were made by flaking the stone under pressure.

places the more recent Wandjinas cover the dynamic figures, but not so often in the northern parts of the Kimberley. Some of the most exciting dynamic figures can be found along the King Edward River.

Heritage value

Aboriginal artwork is not found only on rock walls. Engravings were also made in pearl shell and wood, and examples of these can be found in the southwest of the Kimberley.

Although many of the traditional ways of the Aborigines have been lost since European colonization, the rock art links today's Aborigines with their ancient culture. The present revival in Aboriginal culture, together with renewed access to traditional lands, is allowing Aborigines to practice some of their traditional ways again, and to pass these on to younger generations. Young Aborigines are being taught the rituals involved in retouching the paintings, ensuring the continuing relationship between the people and their ancestral lands.

European explorers

The Dutch

The first European infiltration into the Kimberley was around 1838, 50 years after the Union Jack was hoisted at Sydney Cove. It took almost another 50 years for Alexander Forrest to open up the region for pastoral and agricultural settlement. Some 200 years before this, however, Portuguese sailors had probably reached the Kimberley coast. Dirk Hartog, a Dutch explorer, is credited with the first recorded encounter in 1616. In 1644 Abel Tasman, another Dutchman, mapped several thousand miles of Australia's coastline, including the Kimberley coast. Tasman's chart, which still exists today, refers to Australia as "Compagnis Nieu Nederland," which later became "New Holland." Although Tasman landed on the Kimberley coast, little is known of his exploits apart from a hostile encounter with Aborigines. The legacy of the Dutch explorers remains in the number of Dutch place names along the Australian coast.

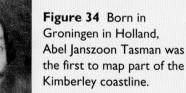

Figure 33 William Dampier set sail on his second voyage to Australia in 1699. Because the start of his voyage was delayed, he sailed via the Cape of Good Hope at the southern tip of South Africa instead of around the southern tip of South America, as he had planned. Had Dampier sailed via South America he would have discovered the east coast of Australia.

Figure 34 Born in Groningen in Holland, Abel Janszoon Tasman was the first to map part of the Kimberley coastline.

(Photos courtesy of National Library of Australia)

The British

The next stage of exploration was left to the British. In 1688, William Dampier sailed through the south seas aboard the buccaneer ship the *Cygnet*. The ship was in need of repairs, so Dampier found a quiet spot on the Kimberley coast. During that time Dampier carefully observed the land and its inhabitants. On his return to England, he wrote *A New Voyage Around The World*, bringing himself considerable fame. He described the land as barren and the Aborigines as the most miserable people in the world. Yet he maintained the hope that somewhere around the shores of New Holland there were fertile lands, and this led to his second voyage in 1699. This voyage, which took Dampier around the northwestern coast of Australia, failed to live up to his hopes. He noticed pearl shells along the west Kimberley coast, little realizing that they would one day give rise to a thriving industry. Australia's uninviting shores held little attraction for the European explorers and traders after this.

Figure 35 (right)   The Cape Leveque lighthouse is a reminder of the dangerous seas around the cape that caused such trouble for the early explorers.

(Photo courtesy of Mike Leonard)

Figure 36 (below)   One of the reasons why early explorers failed to find the Ord River was because it flows into Cambridge Gulf. This gulf has many arms (inlets), and each arm looks as though it could be the mouth of a river. This view across Cambridge Gulf shows an area known as the False Mouths of the Ord.

(Photo courtesy of Mike Leonard)

The French

A number of French explorers also found their way to Australia. Nicolaus Baudin set off from France in 1800 with his ships *Le Geographe* and *Le Naturaliste*. The purpose of Baudin's expedition was to map the Australian coast and carry out scientific observations. However, he rushed along the Australian coastline, making exploration impossible for the scientists on board. His only remaining contribution is the number of French place names along the coast, including the Bonaparte Archipelago and the Joseph Bonaparte Gulf. From that time on, exploration was to remain firmly in the hands of the British colonists.

(Photo courtesy of Maria Mann)

Figure 37   Cape Leveque is the northern tip of the Dampier Peninsula in the western Kimberley. It is one of the many places bearing a French name along the west coast of Australia. This aerial view shows the sandstone cliffs and the beaches.

Exploring the ragged coast

If you look at a map of Australia you will find no coastline more ragged than the Kimberley coast. Some of the strongest waves on the planet batter this coastline from time to time. The dangerous seas constantly impeded exploration and settlement in this remote area, and sometimes resulted in the deaths of those brave or foolish enough to attempt more than a quick look. The explorers' hope was to find a river that would allow convenient inland exploration and provide a source of fresh water. But the vast coastline was not an easy one to chart.

Phillip Parker King

In 1818 Phillip Parker King set off for the Kimberley on board the *Mermaid*. His aim was to chart the coastline, and he succeeded in discovering Cambridge Gulf at the mouth of the Ord River. King failed to find the river itself because he did not venture far enough into the gulf.

In the southwest corner of the Kimberley, King also examined the islands and shoreline of Cygnet Bay (later renamed King Sound). Disaster Bay reminds us of the occasion when violent seas almost claimed King's ship. Encounter Bay recalls a skirmish King and his men had with Aborigines, in which injuries occurred but no one was killed.

(Photo courtesy of Mike Leonard)

George Grey and John Stokes

In 1837, Lieutenant George Grey sailed aboard the *Lynher* to Hanover Bay on the west coast of the Kimberley. From there he was to travel overland, following the coast toward the new colony in the southwest of Australia, in the hope of finding great rivers—a huge undertaking. Before setting out, Grey and his companions claimed the land for Britain, and hoisted the flag. Supplies were brought ashore and the journey

(Photo courtesy of Rodney Paterson)

Figure 38 (above)   The Forrest River is named after the explorer Alexander Forrest (see page 30). This peculiar black river flows west from the Pseudomys Hills in the northern Kimberley into Cambridge Gulf. This picture is taken near the Oombulgurri Mission. It is completely inaccessible by road.

Figure 39 (left)   The King George Falls in the far north of the Kimberley cascade off a plateau directly into the ocean. This is the daunting coastline that the early explorers had to contend with when trying to move into the interior of northwestern Australia.

Figure 40 Sponsored by the Royal Geographical Society, Sir George Grey was the first European explorer to travel inland into the Kimberley. He reached as far as the Glenelg and Sale Rivers. Grey intended to return to the Kimberley at a later time, but became involved in politics.

(Photo courtesy of National Library of Australia)

began. Deep gorges forced Grey inland, and at one stage of the journey he and a couple of companions were attacked by Aborigines. An Aborigine drove a spear into Grey's hip. Grey retaliated by firing his gun, killing the man. Two weeks later the party continued their journey south. Grey wrote of the land that he had seen "no scenery to equal it."

Accompanying the *Lynher* was the *Beagle*, the ship which had transported Charles Darwin on his famous voyages. Aboard the *Beagle*, Lieutenant John Stokes and his exploration team discovered the 340-mile-long Fitzroy River that had eluded Grey. Despite strong currents, Stokes' team was able to sail 22 miles up the river in a small boat.

Grey did discover two smaller rivers, the Glenelg and the Sale on the central west coast, which were to be the location of early attempts by Europeans to settle the Kimberley.

Opening up the land

The discoveries on the Kimberley's west coast did not lead to any permanent British settlements. Bad weather, poor pasture, and resistance by Aborigines defending their land ruined all efforts. It was not until 1879 that one of the great rivers of the Kimberley—a vital source of fresh water in the inland plains—was discovered.

Alexander Forrest

In 1879, Alexander Forrest journeyed along the Fitzroy River on horseback with his nine companions, one of whom wrote that the banks were covered with "eucalyptus, banksia, and acacias. Ducks, turkeys, and cockatoos were there in countless numbers."

They headed northeast until they were stopped by the impenetrable King Leopold Range. They changed to a northwest direction, but were again forced back to the Fitzroy River. Forrest then turned east, trying to reach the Overland Telegraph more than 340 miles away. This took him into unknown territory where he soon discovered great grassy plains and the 310-mile-long Ord, the great river of the eastern Kimberley. These discoveries opened the way for European settlement.

Figure 41 With pastoral land in southern and eastern Australia growing scarce, Alexander Forrest's 1879 expedition into the Kimberley was vital in providing almost 25 million acres of pasture.

(Photo courtesy of National Library of Australia)

Forrest's discovery was used by the Western Australian government to promote the Kimberley region for grazing. One million acres of land could be claimed for as little as two shillings and sixpence (about 60 cents). By 1883, more than 50 million acres had been leased.

The "Cattle Kings"

Pastoralists in the eastern colonies, thousands of miles away, were keen to lay their claims to land, but then came the enormous challenge of getting their stock to the Kimberley. This led to epic cattle drives across the Australian continent, and to an era of cattle-grazing families running huge properties. These families became known as the "Cattle Kings."

From Goulburn in New South Wales, the MacDonald brothers set off in 1883 with 670 cattle and 36 bullocks to fulfill the dream of their father who died shortly before the epic journey began. Their million acres, known as Fossil Downs, lay on the Fitzroy River near present-day Fitzroy Crossing. They arrived three years and 3400 miles later, after the world's longest cattle drive. Their bullock wagon is said to be the first vehicle to have crossed the vast expanse of inland Australia.

Figure 42 The King Leopold Range stretches southeast from Walcott Inlet on the Indian Ocean to the Fitzroy River. This is the mountain range that caused Alexander Forrest serious problems in his attempt to cross the Kimberley from west to east. European settlement in the Kimberley did not occur until Forrest managed to skirt around this range and discover the great grassy plains of the Ord River.

Two years earlier, Irish-born pioneer Nat Buchanan had taken up his land in the southern parts of the eastern Kimberley, bringing with him several thousand head of cattle. The Buchanan Highway, named after him, follows part of his route.

Perhaps the most famous of the "Cattle King" families is the Duracks. In 1883, the family set off from Cooper Creek in Queensland with thousands of cattle and two years later they set up the Argyle, Ivanhoe, Lissadell, and Dunham River stations along the Ord River in the Kimberley. Their epic story is told in Dame Mary Durack's book *Kings in Grass Castles*. For over 100 years the Duracks held land in the Kimberley. An era ended when they sold off the last of their properties in 1989.

Figure 43 It is difficult for us to imagine the incredible cattle drives to the Kimberley that took place in the late 1800s. But the cattle kings achieved their goal, driving hundreds of cattle over thousands of miles through the humid wet season as well as the dusty dry. Some of these drives were the longest in the history of any country.

Gold rush

The European settlement of the Kimberley received a major boost with the discovery of gold along the Fitzroy River. The government had offered a reward of £5000 (about $10,000) for the first person who discovered gold, and prospectors roamed the colony. In 1885, Charles Hall and John Slattery unearthed 10.5 ounces of gold at the site that became known as Halls Creek, and claimed the reward.

Within a year, 2000 prospectors were searching the goldfield. Overall, up to 10,000 people may have passed through the area. But the conditions were very tough and excitement soon gave way to disappointment. The amount of gold found never met the expectations of the diggers. Some died on the long journey to the field; others arrived only to find many diggers were leaving, disappointed and empty-handed. Even Hall and Slattery missed out: the government refused them the reward on the grounds that the goldfield never produced the required amount of gold. It is difficult to know just how

(Photo courtesy of Mike Leonard)

Figure 44 In the town of Halls Creek, this statue has been erected to remember the pioneers of the Kimberley. In particular, this statue tells the story of Russian Jack, a gold prospector who carried a sick friend in a bush wheelbarrow more than 180 miles from Halls Creek to Wyndham in search of medical aid.

(Photo courtesy of Maria Mann)

much the field really did produce, as the government tax on gold meant that many diggers left the field with their finds hidden in their bags.

What the gold rush did do was to lay the foundation upon which a community could be built. Police stations had been established, a postal service was in operation, and the telegraph linked the region to Perth, the most important

Figure 45 The ruins of the Lillimooloora police station remind us that the Kimberley has not always been the peaceful place it is today. The police established themselves here in the late 1800s to keep law and order at a time when there was much fighting between the station owners and the Aborigines, whose people had lived in the land for thousands of years.

city in Western Australia. If gold had not been discovered, the small population would have been waiting many years to receive any of these services.

(Photo courtesy of Wilson Barr)

Figure 46

The Royal Flying Doctor Service

The Royal Flying Doctor Service was started in 1928 by Reverend John Flynn of the Australian Inland Mission. As radio technology improved, even those living in the most remote regions of the country could be in instant contact with a doctor. In homesteads throughout the Kimberley, the Royal Flying Doctor Service of Australia medical chest is kept close to the radio so that the doctor can give treatment over the air. Much of the Flying Doctor's work is now preventative, such as the clinics held in remote Aboriginal communities. Royal Flying Doctor bases are located at Wyndham and Derby, where there are also hospitals. If a situation is particularly serious, the patient can be flown to Perth.

Mining the Kimberley

Land in the Kimberley is used for many different purposes, including mining, farming, fishing, and recreation. Mining is a fast-growing industry with lots of potential, but the precious and unique Kimberley environment must be protected. In some cases, new technology is needed before it will be economic to extract the known mineral reserves.

There have already been several successful mines in the Kimberley. Yampi Sound, about 80 miles north of Derby, is one of the world's richest iron ore deposits. Cockatoo Island was the first mine in the sound, producing 34 million tons of ore between 1951 and 1986. Mining company BHP has just completed another iron ore project on Koolan Island. This iron ore mine operated from 1965 and produced about 4.2 million tons per year.

Some of the future possibilities for mining in the Kimberley include natural gas in the Bonaparte Basin, lead and zinc in the Sorby Hills northeast of Kununurra, and nickel to the southwest of Kununurra. Huge deposits of bauxite on the Mitchell Plateau and at Cape Bougainville could also be mined to produce aluminum.

The Argyle diamond mine

One well-known mine still operating in the Kimberley is the Argyle diamond mine, famous for its beautiful pink diamonds. It was the first diamond mine in Australia and is also the world's largest. Most of the diamonds mined are of industrial or near-gem quality, but about 5 percent rank among the finest diamonds in the world. Blood-red diamonds are the rarest of all, and pinks are almost as rare. Argyle is the only mine in the world to regularly produce pink diamonds. Many other Argyle diamonds are bronze or yellow in color.

Figure 47 Open-cut mining of iron ore has ravaged the once-spectacular Koolan Island, which lies in the Buccaneer Archipelago, directly north of Derby.

The mine was discovered in late 1979 in a valley at the foot of the Ragged Range. First the alluvial diamonds were excavated from the gravel bed of Smoke Creek, but before long a huge open-cut mine was established to get at the actual ore containing the precious minerals.

The ore deposit is immense, and it also has an unusual feature. Prior to the discovery of the Argyle mine, it was thought that diamonds were found only in a type of rock called "kimberlite." However, the Argyle mine contains a different type of rock, known as "lamproite." The Argyle mine was the first lamproite diamond mine in the world.

Figure 48 (right) The Argyle mine produces many exotically colored diamonds, but the most prized of all are the rare "Argyle pinks." Out of every 10 tons of diamonds mined, there would not be enough pink diamonds to fill a cup.

Figure 49 (above) The discovery of four small diamonds along the shores of Smoke Creek in 1979 was to lead geologists to the world's largest source of the precious gems. The Argyle diamond mine, a mile long and up to 2000 feet wide in places, is studded with billions of small diamonds.

Pearl farms

There are two large pearl farms in the Kimberley, one at Kuri Bay, north of Derby, and the other at Cygnet Bay in King Sound. A natural pearl occurs when an oyster tries to eliminate an irritant – such as a grain of sand – from inside its shell. When it cannot get rid of the problem, the oyster will cover it with layer after layer of "nacre," which forms the pearl. On a pearl farm, artificial irritants are inserted inside the oyster shells and the oysters are prevented from rejecting them. About 18 months later the pearl will be ready.

Kimberley cattle

Although the days of the Kimberley "Cattle Kings" might be over, most of this region is still closely connected with cattle. Around 87,000 square miles (nearly 60 percent) of the Kimberley is devoted to the pastoral industry, in spite of the fact that less than 10 percent is considered to be high-quality grazing land. This area supports 99 leases and 600,000 head of cattle.

Cattle stations occupy the grasslands and open woodlands of the Kimberley. The need to care for these environments is a growing issue in the region. Cattle are selective grazers, meaning that they prefer certain types of plants over others. When they eat these plants they change the ecological balance of the area. When the grass gets too dry, the cattle will start eating "top feed" from bushes and trees.

The grazing land is owned by the government and is leased to station owners for a specific period of time. These lease owners, or the managers who run the station for them, graze cattle for beef. Freighting cattle to the markets from such a remote region is very expensive, and the unpredictable climate is an added strain on the industry. Many landowners have had to sell up over the years, and the present trend in the Kimberley is toward fewer owners with larger properties.

The pastoral industry requires a large number of different skills. Vets, truck drivers, and fence and road builders are needed as well as the managers, ringers, and meat packing plant

(Photo courtesy of Keren Francis)

workers. Because fence building is difficult and costly, the Kimberley pastoral industry has tended to be open range. This means that the cattle roam all over the Kimberley grazing lands and are rounded up each year by ringers on horses, in helicopters or planes, or in four-wheel-drive vehicles. Some stations use trap yards. The cattle enter the yard through special gates to get at the water and hay inside, and then find that they cannot get out.

Once the cattle are rounded up, the station

(Photo courtesy of Department of Foreign Affairs and Trade)

Figure 51 (left) Station managers have to take care of their cattle by making sure they have enough water and food, by preventing disease, and by warding off dingoes, which kill calves and young cattle for food. Poisoned baits are sometimes laid to kill the dingoes.

Figure 50 (above) In the Kimberley, cattle range over huge areas of land. To round up the cattle over such vast distances, planes and helicopters are sometimes used.

workers can dehorn and brand them. The cattle may also be weighed and vaccinated against diseases before being loaded onto trucks for transport to the markets. A lot of Kimberley cattle are shipped live to Asia where they are slaughtered in accordance with particular religious principles. Others are sold to Australian packing plants or to farmers in the south of the state.

Figure 52

(Photo courtesy of Keren Francis)

Feral cattle

Cattle have become a problem in the Kimberley because of the open-range style of farming. Thousands of wild cattle roam the region, and when they get into deep canyons or thick rain forest, they are very difficult to round up. Their grazing and trampling does a great deal of damage to the environment and can lead to erosion. They also compete with native animals for food. When this occurs in fragile ecosystems, such as the margins along the arid regions, it can cause a complete change in the environment and also deplete native animal populations.

Kimberley crops

Initially the Kimberley pasture was used only for grazing cattle and sheep. In 1937, Kimberley Durack of the Argyle Downs station started experimenting with crops near the Behn River. Five years later, the state government established its own experimental farm on the Ord River. At first, irrigation was used to enable crops such as cotton, sorghum, and corn to grow. Then it was proposed that a dam could be built on the Ord River to trap the huge flow of water during the wet season for use in the dry.

Figure 53 In southern areas sunflowers are grown during the summer, but on the Ord sunflowers are a winter crop.

The Ord River Irrigation Area

During the dry season, the Ord River trickles its way through the western Kimberley. In the wet, however, this trickle becomes a raging torrent. By controlling this flow, much of the dry land around the Ord could be irrigated.

In 1941, the Western Australian government began experimenting with the river to test its potential, but it was not until 1963 that the Ord River Project, which included the building of a dam, was set in operation. The Ord River Dam created Lake Argyle, which provides water to more than 175,000 acres of land.

(Photo courtesy of Mike Leonard)

(Photo courtesy of Mike Leonard)

Figure 54 Lake Argyle is Australia's largest reservoir. It is nine times bigger than Sydney Harbor.

Problems

Much of the pasture in the region had been overgrazed, so in 1967 the State government took back the leases and started a rehabilitation project. Without this action, thousands of tons of silt would have washed into Lake Argyle every wet season.

Figure 55 Irrigation allows many different types of crops to grow along the Ord River: mangoes, grapefruit, lemons, bananas, rockmelons, watermelons, grapes, asparagus, and many other vegetables and grains.

At its fullest, the lake spreads out over 770 square miles and supports all sorts of wildlife including freshwater crocodiles. In the process, the town of Kununurra was born and the Durack homestead had to be moved to avoid being drowned by the new lake. Today the homestead is a museum.

At first, the main crops grown were cotton and, when that failed, rice. A combination of diseases, pests, tough markets, transport expenses, and the removal of government subsidies put an end to these efforts. What was needed were crops that brought high returns, so that the project could pay its own way. This led to experimentation with cashews, peanuts, chick peas, bananas, and rockmelons.

Today the Ord River Project is doing very well. It concentrates on a wide range of tree and field crops, including mangoes, melons, bananas, corn, and beans. One of the newest crops is sugarcane, and indications are that it is going to become a multimillion dollar industry.

Kimberley towns

Broome—pearl of the Kimberley

In November 1883, Sir Frederick Napier Broome, then the Governor of Western Australia, wrote to the Colonial Secretary complaining about the decision to name a town in the far north after him. "[It] is likely to remain a mere 'dummy' townsite inhabited by the tenants of three graves," he wrote. But by the next decade the little town, which had been created to provide a port for the industries of the west Kimberley, had found a new calling—pearls.

The pearl industry boomed—especially in the production of mother-of-pearl, which was used in cutlery handles, buttons, and ornaments —and Broome remains one of the most important pearling centers in the world. At first it was local Aborigines who took on the perilous task of diving for oyster shells, but before long they were being replaced by divers from Malaysia, Indonesia, and Japan. The present inhabitants of Broome, who number around 7000, are largely descendants of these early adventurers. Broome's Chinatown, and its street signs written in English, Malaysian, Chinese, Japanese, and Arabic, are a reminder of the town's multicultural past and present.

(Photo courtesy of Ken Stepnell)

Figure 56 A Japanese gravestone at the Broome cemetery is a reminder of the many pearl divers of different nationalities who lost their lives in the early days of the pearling industry.

The pearling industry has changed a great deal since the early days. There have been technological improvements in diving, and cultured pearls (pearls "farmed" in oyster beds) are replacing the extremely rare, naturally occurring pearls.

Derby—gateway to the gorges

From the time of the early pastoralists the sprawling port of Derby has been the market and administrative center of west Kimberley, first for the cattle industry and now increasingly for the mining industries.

The Lurrujarri trail

The Aboriginal heritage of the area is preserved in the Lurrujarri trail that has been established along the coast north of Broome. This trail follows an Aboriginal song cycle which is part of a larger Dreaming track that begins in the Kimberley and ends at Uluru (Ayers Rock). The trail, starting at Minarringy and ending 50 miles south at Minyirr (Gantheaume Point), interprets the coast and its flora and fauna, as well as describing how they are used by the Aboriginal people.

However, Derby is not all business. It is also known as the "Gateway to the Gorges," referring in particular to the spectacular Geikie and Windjana Gorges which have been protected within national parks. Also nearby is an Aboriginal heritage trail—the Pigeon Heritage Trail—which has been established to allow visitors to follow the adventures of a famous nineteenth century Aboriginal named Jundumurra, or Pigeon (see page 23).

Figure 58 (right)   Every August there is a pearl festival known as "Shinju Matsuri" which acknowledges Broome's debt to the Japanese pearlers.

Figure 57 (above)   Broome has an unusual cultural mix of Aborigines and people of Indonesian, Filipino, Malaysian, Japanese, Chinese, and European descent. This house is a typical example of those found in the Chinatown area of Broome.

On the road

The region's main road link is the Great Northern Highway, which sweeps in a huge arc along the southern edge of the Kimberley, joining Broome in the southwest with Wyndham and Kununurra in the northeast. Beginning in Derby is the other main route, the Gibb River Road, which cuts directly across the Kimberley. It was originally built to serve the cattle industry, and it is flanked on either side by huge cattle stations. It also gives access to a number of national parks and Aboriginal lands.

Australia's top towns

In the far northeast is Wyndham, sandwiched between the tidal mangrove flats that line the coast of Cambridge Gulf (where crocodiles are not uncommon) and the hills of the Bastion Range. Like Derby, Wyndham is a port town

(Photo courtesy of Mike Leonard)

Figure 59 Wyndham is actually two towns about 3 miles apart. When there was no more room near the port, people settled farther inland at a place that became known as Three Miles.

built for the cattle industry, although during the 1880s it also served the goldfields at Halls Creek. The main street is lined with baobab trees as old as the town itself, and many of the town's early buildings still stand. The panoramic view from the nearby Five Rivers Lookout takes in the port and the five rivers around it (the Ord, King, Pentecost, Forrest, and Durack).

Just south of Wyndham is Kununurra, the last town before the Northern Territory border. Kununurra was built during the 1960s as part of the Ord River Project and it has largely replaced Wyndham as the main town in the east Kimberley.

"Kununurra" is the Aboriginal word for "big waters," and refers to nearby Lake Argyle, a huge artificial lake created when the Ord River was dammed for the Ord River Irrigation Project. Plane or helicopter trips from Kununurra take visitors over the lake as well as to the spectacular Bungle Bungle Range.

The Great Northern Highway

Of the tiny towns that dot the Great Northern Highway, the largest are Halls Creek (population 1350) and Fitzroy Crossing (population 1200). Old Halls Creek—the site of feverish activity during the gold rush—now lies in ruins. The present town was established about 9 miles away when it became necessary to find a more

Figure 60 (above) In 1948, the people of Halls Creek voted to move the gold rush town to a new site, closer to fresh water supplies. Now it awaits a new rush of people.

Kandimalal

Djaru Aborigines have a story that describes how two rainbow snakes created the Sturt and Wolfe Creeks as they traveled across the desert. When one of these snakes first emerged from the ground, it formed the huge crater called Kandimalal.

Figure 61 The Kalumburu Aboriginal community live in the northernmost part of the Kimberley.

reliable water supply. About 90 miles farther south, on the edge of the Great Sandy Desert, is the Wolfe Creek meteorite crater, the second largest meteorite crater in the world.

Fitzroy Crossing sits at the foot of the hills of the Geikie Gorge National Park, with the floodplains of the Fitzroy River spreading out toward the west. The town's population swells enormously during the dry season as thousands of tourists pass through. The mainly Aboriginal inhabitants live along the banks of the river toward Geikie Gorge. During the dry season, this river is reduced to a series of waterholes, but during the wet season enough water flows to fill Sydney Harbor every five hours.

Environmental issues

The Kimberley is home to many different plant and animal species. Rare whales and turtles live in the warm seas off the coast; several endangered bat species, such as the ghost bat, live in caves in the gorges; and thousands of birds, including peregrine falcons and gouldian finches, build their homes in the trees or by the water.

Inland waterways provide refuge for the freshwater and saltwater crocodiles, as well as many different species of fish, including the rare pygmy rainbow fish. Bilbies, marsupial mice, the rare rock ringtail possum, and about 40 other species of small Australian mammals survive in the Kimberley because it is remote from the feral cats and other pests that have destroyed their habitats elsewhere.

No extinctions have been recorded in the Kimberley since European settlement, but cattle grazing has contributed to the dwindling numbers of many of the plants and animals, such as the golden bandicoot and the golden-backed tree-rat. Feral horses and cattle are problems, but it is the feral donkey that causes most destruction in the Kimberley. Donkeys were first introduced into the area during the gold rushes in the late 1800s. They now congregate in huge herds, and their grazing, trampling, and domination of waterholes damages the environment and menaces the native fauna. Although thousands are shot each year, their numbers have not been greatly reduced.

It is estimated that less than a quarter of the Kimberley—the area between Walcott Inlet, Mt Elizabeth, and the Drysdale River—has escaped environmental damage. Only 4 percent of the region is protected by national parks or nature reserves. Although many new sites have been suggested, very little has been done to protect them. The conservation question must be resolved if the future of the unique Kimberley environment is to be ensured.

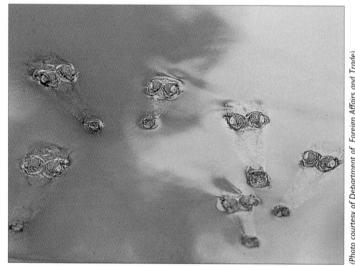

(Photo courtesy of Department of Foreign Affairs and Trade)

Figure 62 Crocodiles are ancient inhabitants of the Kimberley. They have lived on Earth for more than 200 million years. Yet only a small percentage of newborn crocodiles reach maturity. Saltwater crocodiles can lay up to 50 eggs, while freshwater crocodiles lay between 13 and 15. Goannas and dingoes prey on the eggs and others are drowned in wet season floods. All in all, no more than 4 percent of all crocodiles survive to adulthood. Crocodiles have a layer of crystals behind the retina in their eyes. This enables them to see at night and it also causes their eyes to glow when a spotlight is pointed at them.

Figure 63 (above)   Many birds are attracted to crops on the Ord during the dry season. They can become pests unless alternative feeding areas are provided for them.

Figure 64 (right)   Donkeys were not common in Australia until 1866 when they were introduced as work or pack animals. Because feral donkeys can change the natural balance of the environment, the government tries to control their numbers.

Figure 65 (left)   On steep rock faces throughout the Kimberley, baobabs grow out of the most unlikely cracks and crevices. This is because of the way the baobab seed is dispersed. Being too heavy to be blown by the wind, the seed is spread in the droppings of the agile rock wallaby. The seeds rest in cracks in the rock until they are germinated by the rain.

A new national park

(Photo courtesy of Mike Leonard)

Figure 66 (left) Over a long period of time Bell Creek has carved away many layers of rock to create Bell Gorge, an idyllic waterway with beautiful falls.

Figure 67 (below) The King Leopold Range, site of the new national park, is home to many rare animals and plants, some of which are unique to the area.

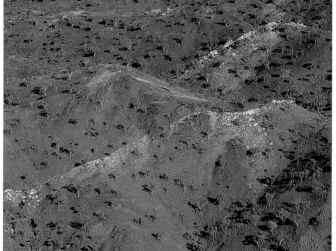

(Photo courtesy of Mike Leonard)

One new national park is being established northwest of Derby on the old Mount Hart pastoral lease. It takes in 925,000 acres and features two incredible gorges—Bell Gorge and Lennard Gorge—in the King Leopold Range, as well as an old station homestead. Bell Creek, lined with baobab trees, winds through the park with a series of waterfalls.

Many rare animals live in the national park, including the brindled bandicoot, rock wallaby, and rock ringtail possum. There are also some rare plants, including a cycad not found anywhere else in Australia, and a rare eucalyptus.

Glossary

alluvial Describes a type of mineral deposit laid down by water, usually found in a creek or river bed.

billabong A pool or lagoon.

boomerang A curved, flat wooden missile, orginally used by Aboriginal peoples when hunting.

bush tucker Edible plants and animals found in the Australian bush. These were often the traditional foods of Aborigines.

Dreamtime In Aboriginal mythology, creation time. A time when ancestral creatures roamed the land, creating the world we see today. The trails they followed are known as Dream trails or tracks.

erosion The wearing away of the land by wind or water.

estuary The wide mouth of a river where it meets the sea.

extinct If a species of animal or plant is extinct, there are no more of that species alive.

feral Domestic animals that have become wild.

glacial period A cold period in the Earth's history when there were many more glaciers.

glacier A mass of ice that moves very slowly across the land.

habitat The area in which an animal or plant naturally lives.

inter-tidal zone The area of coast that is dry at low tide and covered by sea at high tide.

irrigation Taking water from a river, lake or dam to use on farm crops.

lease The agreement made when land or a dwelling is rented for a particular purpose and length of time.

mesa A flat-topped rock platform.

meteorite A rock from outer space that falls to Earth.

nomadic Moving from one place to another, usually in search of food.

open range Unfenced grazing land.

Pangaea "All lands." The supercontinent that existed until 200 million years ago. It was a single land mass composed of all the present-day continents.

pastoralist A person who grazes livestock, such as cattle, usually on a large property.

pasture Grassland used for grazing animals.

rainforest Dense forest consisting of several layers, or canopies, of trees. Rainforests occur mainly in areas of high rainfall.

ringer A station worker who helps with mustering and other cattle work.

sediment Fine particles of soil or rock that are carried by water and eventually settle to the bottom.

selective grazing Where grazing animals eat only one or a few types of plants and not other types in the same area.

spinifex A type of spiny grass that grows in large clumps, common in outback Australia.

tributary River or stream that feeds into a larger stream.

wallaby Native Australian animal. Some resemble small kangaroos, others are more like possums.

Index